Herd

DANIEL BOONE'S
ECHO

DANIEL BOONE'S ECHO

WILLIAM O. STEELE

Illustrated by *Nicolas*

HARCOURT, BRACE & WORLD, INC., NEW YORK

One

Does and fawns lifted their heads and sniffed the air. There was somebody coming!

Bears scrambled up tree trunks to get a good look. There was somebody coming!

A flock of turkeys scurried across the trail. There was somebody coming!

Three flighty young turkeys got confused and ran straight down the trail right at that somebody!

"Purdy, purdy, purdy!" they called and flapped their wings in fright.

And Daniel Boone laughed and waved his old black hat.

"Oh, no," he cried. "I ain't purty. I'm ugly as sin, I reckon, but it don't bother me none, for this is a fine May morning and calico bushes are blooming and birds are singing. And I've been in the wilderness where no white man has stepped before, and mighty few red men. So I'll thank you to step aside, young turkeys, and I'll just travel on through Cumberland Gap."

Daniel went along and along, and as he went he sang:

"Oh, I've been off to Kentuckee,
Been there and headed back.
My feet are so tired of walking,
I tote them in a sack.

My shot bag's crawled into my ear,
I'm lost as I can be,
And I will drown the buffalo
In the water on my knee.

My rifle's tied in bowknots,
All my powder's in my hair.
And with my trusty moccasin
I'll shoot that sassy bear."

And it was not long till he came to Cumberland Gap, and out he went on the other side. Once he stopped to drink from a clear cold spring. And once he stopped to look around him, for in May the world is so beautiful, a man must look at it often or he won't believe it.

By and by he came to the trading store at Pumpkin Grove. And inside there was a heap of men, tall men with tall rifles. Some were buying powder and lead, some were trading deerskins for knives and hatchets, but most were just standing around talking.

The proprietor's name was Evan Dunkle, and unless he wore a coonskin cap, he'd not a hair upon his head. He sprang smack up out of the bolts of calico and barrels of brown lump sugar when he saw Daniel coming.

"Boys," he cried. "It's spring for certain-sure. Last week I saw the geese a-headed north, and today I spy Dan'l's old black hat, and that's the surest sign of all."

"Howdy!" whooped Daniel. "Evan, I see them Injuns has not brought back your hair yet. It's a crying shame to think of your poor old scalp living so lonely and far off amongst the Shawnee."

"Now, Dan'l, you never come here to tell me I was bald-headed," said Evan. "What is your business this time? Is it powder you're wanting or a new ax head? Be it lead or salt or meal or a three-legged skillet?"

"It's none of them things I'm here for," Daniel answered. "What I'm after this time is brave hearts and strong arms, for I have it in mind to head straight back to Kentuck and start a settlement there. And I need a heap of good men to go with me."

And Daniel looked at the men who had crowded up around him, and he saw that there was something wrong. Not a soul looked him in the eye. Not one spoke up hearty to say, "I'll go with you, Dan'l."

But Daniel wasn't downhearted. "These folks just don't know about Kentuck," he said to himself. "So I must tell them what a fine, fair place it is."

He smiled at them. "Boys, you ought to see the rich land in Kentuck. Why, the dirt's so rich there, a man dassent go barefoot for fear the dirt will make his feet grow too big to squeeze into his moccasins. And you know a body could raise the finest kind of corn with dirt like that."

Nobody said a thing. Finally one old man hollered out, "There's other things to think of than corn."

"Well, I hope to tell there is," Daniel nodded. "But don't you worry none. There's plenty of cane in Kentuck to feed the horses, and there's trees all over the place to make logs for cabins. And grass—great day in the morning, you should see the grass that grows there. That grass is so big, it'd take three of your cows to chew off one blade."

And he grinned, though the fact was he didn't think it was a very funny joke. Nobody grinned back.

"And there's a heap of game in Kentuck," Daniel went on. "There's so much game, there ain't hardly room to stand. It's got so crowded there, the buck deer ain't got room enough to sprout antlers, and they have to tote their horns in their arms, the way human folks do their rifles and axes."

And this time he laughed fit to bust.

But nobody laughed with him.

"Boys," cried Daniel, when he'd wiped the tears away. "It ain't just the fine game and the rich ground that makes me hone for Kentuck. Kentuck is the fairest land on earth, with green savannas and blue hills and tall trees and wide rivers and the sweetest springs everywhere. A body might live in Kentuckee forever with a happy heart. Now who'll go with me to make a settlement there?"

The men shook their heads. And Daniel looked in each face and saw that the men were really afraid, and he had nothing more to say to them. He felt his heart sink down as far as his knees.

"No, thank ye kindly, Dan'l," said one man at last. "I'll not go to Kentuckee, nor any of these others. Why, not even Injuns will live in Kentuckee. It's full of queer critters and dangerous varmints."

"That it is, for a fact," a man standing behind Daniel began. "I know there's a thing living in Kentuck called a Sling-Tailed Galootis. This Galootis is flat and wider than it is long, and its jaws don't go up and down. No, sir, its mouth opens sideways, and it can't eat nothing that is standing up straight. Its mouth ain't made that way. Nature has fixed a sling on its tail, a sort of leather pocket that can hold a rock pretty as you please. And when the Galootis hunts for food, it gallops along whirling its tail

over its head, and when it finds a man, it slings that rock at him and knocks him down so he's lying out all straight along the ground. And then the Galootis stretches its mouth sideways and rolls the man right inside. Ohhhh, the Galootis is a horrible beast!"

The listeners all shivered and shook. But Daniel stood

there straight and firm as a red oak tree and wondered mightily.

Another man spoke up. "I've heared tell there was great old holes in the ground—the burrows of something bigger than a log cabin. And sometimes you can see the critter's smoking breath rise up out of the holes."

"I had a neighbor once told me about the One-Horned Sumpple. Said it was the worst varmint in Kentuck," another went on. "The Sumpple's got one horn on its head which is hollow clean through from one end t'other. And it'll run up to a man, quick as scat, and blow dust through that horn into a man's eyes, so a body can't see to run away. And while you're good and blinded, it comes and eats you, piece by piece."

He shook his head, all solemn and sober. "I wouldn't take my wife and young 'uns to a place where such things live for money!"

"Oh, there's monstrous big somethings living all over Kentuck, Dan'l," cried Evan Dunkle. "I knowed a man once who saw their bones all a-laying round a salt lick. Said the varmint's very toe bones was as big as tables. Said a man and his wife and six little ones could live inside the beastie's ribs and never be crowded."

"Oh, them varmints," said Daniel, and he grinned,

for he had seen those bones his very own self. "Why, they're all dead. A bunch of bones never yet got up and bit anybody."

"Now how come you to be so sure them varmints are all dead?" somebody asked. "It may be they're hiding in the hills waiting till enough folks come along to make a decent meal. No country looks fair to a man when he's been chewed up real fine. No, Dan'l, I'll stay right here, for I don't mind hard work or cold weather or Injun fighting. But I do mind a monstrous big something most terribly."

Daniel rubbed his chin and looked thoughtful. He was a mite discouraged, but he had no notion of giving up. He'd settle Kentuck some day or split wide open trying. But now he saw he'd best go at this thing in a slantindicular fashion.

"Well, if that's the way you be," he said, "I won't try to change you none. But I got a little plan I might tell of, if'n you are willing to listen."

"Oh, we'll listen, Dan'l," replied one of the men. The others nodded.

"This here is it, then," Daniel told them. "Let one man come with me, just one man. And him and me will go to Kentuck and stay there one year. If we see any dangerous critters, we'll kill 'em. And if that man comes back safe and sound with not so much as one finger missing, then you know that Kentuck is a fine safe land, fit for anybody to live in."

"That seems fair enough to me," admitted Evan Dunkle. "Who'll go with Dan'l? Speak up! Ben Lowry, will you go?"

"I would if I didn't have the sickest kind of horse," said Ben. "I've got to stay close and nurse him all day and all night and in between times too."

"How 'bout you, Bill Sickles?" asked Daniel.

"No, no," cried Bill. "My wife won't let me stir from home."

"I didn't know you was married," Daniel said.

"Oh, I ain't, but I will be, just as soon as I can find somebody to have me," Bill told him, running out the door.

"Then how about Caspar Means?" asked Daniel.

"Nay," answered Caspar. "There's a terrible great hole in my roof, and every time it rains, I must watch the bucket that stands under it so it won't get too full and wet the puncheon floor."

And all the others answered the same way. And now Daniel really began to feel low-spirited.

Finally a lad named Aaron Adamsale stepped up to Daniel. He was big for his age, but his knees shook just a little and his teeth chattered a mite.

"Now, Dan'l Boone, I may be brave and I may not," said Aaron. "I don't rightly know what I am. But I reckon I'll go with you anyhow, for my mammy says I'm too young to know what to be afeared of and this looks like a good time to learn."

Daniel jumped up into the air and clapped his heels together sharply, a thing he was very good at doing. "Oh, young Aaron, you're right!" shouted Daniel. "You're a good lad, and the first lesson to learn is not to stay home and trouble over varmints that may not be there a-tall. So fetch your gear and we'll set out."

Two

So Daniel and Aaron went west down the trail at a right good pace. It was May, and they walked under the yellow flowers of the poplar trees. The air was sweet as fresh milk, and the sky was blue and clear as Daniel's eyes.

But the closer they got to Kentuck, the more Aaron's knees shook, until finally he was shaking all over like he had the ague.

"Oh, this will never do," said Daniel to himself, "for if'n he keeps a-trembling like this, Aaron will shake the ears right off his head. And I've promised to bring him back to Pumpkin Grove safe and sound."

So he took Aaron by the arm and spoke to him in a

soothing fashion. "Now, looky yonder, Aaron," Daniel remarked. "Them's the Cumberland Mountains, and ain't they a fair pretty sight?"

"Oh, indeed they are," answered Aaron, "for I see they are as high as heaven and all them queer varmints will have to stay in Kentuck forever. They could never git over such high mountains and come to Pumpkin Grove."

And he turned around and started walking back the way he had come.

"Now where are you headed?" cried Daniel. "If you aim to go to Kentuck that way, you must travel clean around the world, and it's a longish journey."

"Well, Dan'l," replied Aaron. "I seen them high, high mountains, and I know I could never get over them, so I reckon I'd best get back home to my mammy. I wouldn't be surprised if she wasn't missing me terrible by this time."

"Oh, now, Aaron," said Daniel, "we don't have to climb them mountains. There is a fine gap ahead, low down in the mountans, and it'll let us through just like a gate in a fence. So come along and I'll tell you a tale."

"Well, I do dearly love a tale," Aaron said, and he stepped along lively with hardly a shake or a shiver.

"There was a time once," began Daniel, "when I was

coming along this very same trail, and I come to the gap,
having it in mind to go on through and make camp on
the far side. But I couldn't get through, for something
was a-blocking my way. And do you know what it was?"

"Tell me what it was," said Aaron, "for you know
I'm too simple to guess."

"Well, it was a 'coon," told Daniel. "A monstrous big
'coon, growed so big and fat he'd got stuck smack in
Cumberland Gap, and he couldn't go forward and he
couldn't go back."

"I got stuck in a chimbley once," said Aaron.

"I didn't hardly know what to do," Daniel went on. "I give him a mighty shove, but he never so much as budged. I grabbed him by the ears and tugged till he squalled, but he stayed stuck fast as ever."

"Oh, sometimes my mammy pulls my ears," cried Aaron.

"I reckon I could have shot the critter," Daniel said. "I could have built me a fire and roasted him right where he was and eaten my way through from his forelegs clean to the rings on his tail. But it would have taken a heap of eating and more time than I had to give. And 'coon ain't hardly my favorite meat."

"Goose is what I favor," Aaron told Daniel. "Oh, there ain't nothing in this world so tastesome and good as goose."

They reached Cumberland Gap, and it was a fine low place to get them through the mountains. And Aaron never so much as stumbled once as he followed Daniel along the trail into the opening.

"Well, I fetched out my thinking cap and put it on, for I had to get that 'coon out of my way," said Daniel. "And by-and-by I got a notion. And I searched around in the woods till I found me a mosquito run."

"A mosquito run!" exclaimed Aaron. "Whatever in the nation is that? I've heared tell of a deer run and a buffalo road, but never in all my days have I ever heared of a mosquito run!"

"Oh, there's a heap of skeeter runs in the woods, if'n you know where to look," Daniel declared. "They look a heap like a deer run, but they have a different smell. The smell's redder and spottier than a deer run."

"Oh," grunted Aaron and scratched his head.

"I made me a snare with a bent sapling and a vine smack in the middle of that mosquito path. Then I waited out of sight in the bushes. And after a longish spell I heared a mosquito come tromping down the run, and then I heared him taking on fierce and I knew I had him in my snare. He was roaring and squealing and humming and hooting till I had to stop up my ears afore I could get close to him."

"I got a deaf uncle," Aaron said. "Can't hardly hear loud thunder."

"Pretty soon that skeeter calmed down a mite, and I went up to him and got a good tight hold on that vine caught around his leg. He kicked and bucked and got riled up something terrible, and once he come right at me with that sharp old bill. But I smacked him up along-

side the head with the flat of my hatchet, and he quit that foolishment and stood real quiet and gentle."

Daniel and Aaron made their way through the gap. There were a few steep places to climb, but Aaron never noticed them. And his legs hardly shook at all.

"I'd made me some harness and tow ropes out of vines. So I harnessed up that mosquito just like a horse, and I tied the ropes around the 'coon. And when everything was ready as I could make it, I gave that mosquito a hard smack on the rump and I hollered loud as ever I could, and that skeeter gave a tree-mendous leap and pulled as hard as ever it knew how. It pulled and strained and kicked and tugged. I had my rifle ready in case that mosquito should take a notion to turn on me, but it had its head set on getting away, and it didn't pay me no mind."

"That's the way I am," remarked Aaron. "Can't think about but one thing at a time."

"Well, it finally hauled off and gave such a jerk I figured it would split itself plumb in two. And that 'coon came loose with a pop like a heavy-loaded rifle-gun going off before daybreak. And for a minute or two there was a confusion of 'coon and skeeter and harness. The mosquito tried to fly off but couldn't with the weight of the 'coon holding him back. It kept trying and stumbling

25

around till I took my knife and cut the ropes. And the skeeter zoomed off then, and the 'coon took off in the other direction like a canebrake afire. And I just laughed and went on my way."

Aaron chuckled as he followed along after Daniel. "That must of been a sizable 'coon," he said.

"Oh, it was, it was," agreed Daniel.

Aaron looked sober. "And you say you pulled it out of Cumberland Gap with just one skeeter?"

"Just one," Daniel nodded.

Aaron glanced around uneasily. "Dan'l," he said, and he moved up close as close to the hunter. "You done told me a falsehood. You said there wasn't no fierce varmints in Kentuckee. Well, I 'low a skeeter big enough to pull that 'coon out of the gap was a mighty fierce and biggish varmint. About as fierce as they come and a heap too big."

And he began to tremble again.

Then Daniel saw he had made a mistake. "Oh, Aaron, I reckon I blowed things up a bit," he cried. "Maybe it was four or five skeeters, I don't rightly remember. It might easily have been ten or twelve mosquitoes. Why, skeeters around here ain't a mite bigger than they are around Pumpkin Grove. Don't hardly weigh nothing when you get 'em plucked and drawed."

Aaron calmed down some then. "Oh, no bigger than that, huh?" he said. "Well, I shouldn't have took on so, for I've killed many a Pumpkin Grove skeeter with my bare fist. I ain't never been scared of them little kind."

So they went along through the wilderness of Kentuck for two days, and though Daniel talked as brave and cheerful as he knew how, Aaron's knees still knocked together so hard and so often they got big corns on them.

Near the end of the second day they came to a green valley where buffalo grazed and birds sang and a river full of fat fish looped its way across the savanna.

"Oh, my body and soul!" exclaimed Aaron suddenly, trying to hide behind Daniel. But this was hard to do, for he was a foot taller and two feet wider than Boone. "Whatever is them things, Dan'l, flying around overhead? Tell me quick, for in a minute I'll be dead with fright and then it'll be too late."

"Oh, them ain't nothing to worry about," answered Daniel with a smile. "Them's just eagles giving the beavers a ride around in the fine evening air. The big things on each side is eagles, and that bump in the middle is the beaver. Two eagles each get 'em a beaver and fly him around a mite in the springtime, for beavers don't

27

have much chance to see the countryside. And you got to admit this here is beautiful country."

"Oh, yes," agreed Aaron, peeping around Daniel. "It's the finest country ever I did see."

"Well, then let's look for a good place to build a cabin," cried Daniel, and he led the way across the valley till he found a good place beside a spring.

Suddenly there was a terrible loud snarl, and a panther came jumping out of the woods. Aaron tried to climb up on Daniel's shoulders and wrap his legs around Daniel's head.

The panther crept closer, and its tail swished back and forth in short jerks.

"Oh, we're done for," moaned Aaron. And he shook so hard Daniel wasn't able to stay on his feet, and they both fell over in the grass.

Daniel got loose from Aaron and took the boy by the shoulders and shoved him into a hollow log lying on the ground nearby. "You stay in there out of the way, till I kill this here painter," Daniel said.

But Aaron came shooting out of the log with eyes as big as piggins.

Daniel grabbed him by the seat of the pants and threw him back into the hollow log, shoving him way up inside. Then Boone turned to get his rifle, for the panther was mighty close by this time.

But Aaron popped right out of that log again. Now Daniel was a mite put out with Aaron. "Whatever is the matter with you?" he hollered. "Why in creation can't you stay in that log safely out of my way?"

"There's a bear in there," Aaron cried out. "And he don't want me with him."

The panther gave a final growl and sprang straight for the two men.

Three

Now Aaron was a mite simple, but not so simple he didn't know what happened to folks who got in the way of panthers. He jumped one way and Daniel jumped the other, and the painter stretched out thin as whang-leather trying to scratch both of them.

Aaron shinned up a little oak tree quicker than you can skin a minnow, and Daniel lit out running through the woods with the panther right behind him. But Daniel was in a bad way, for he had laid his rifle down by the hollow log.

"I might could use my knife," mused Daniel. "I could turn around and stick this here painter with my knife."

And then he thought about how close he'd have to get

to that panther to use his knife. He thought about the panther's great big old paws and its sharp old talons and its huge biting teeth. And he thought maybe he wouldn't try to stick the panther.

"My knife's got such a fine cutting edge on it," Daniel told himself, "I reckon I won't dull it none by carving up a painter."

So he kept right on running.

He leaped over huckleberry bushes and he dodged around sourwood trees. Once he ran past the oak tree Aaron had climbed, and he couldn't help admiring how much the boy looked like an acorn hanging there.

Now all the time Daniel was running and jumping and dodging, he kept right on thinking too, which shows what a very fine fellow he was. As he ran by the hollow log, he thought about trying to hide inside it.

"No," he told himself. "I'd best not, for there's a fierce bear in there. And I ain't no more in the notion of bear-fighting than I am of painter-fighting."

In a spell he ran by the hollow log again. And this time he thought what a fine thing it would be if the *panther* was in the notion for a little bear-fighting, for Daniel was getting mighty tired of having that panther breathe hot and heavy on his neck.

"I believe I could kind of persuade the painter to fight," he thought. "And it would sure be a shame not to get two such good fellows together."

So the third time around he knew exactly what to do. He ran right smack at the opening of the log, and just as he reached it, he leaped way up into the air. And the panther went scooting underneath him, straight into the log, as neat and tidy as a knife into a sheath, for the animal was going too fast to stop.

"Quick!" Daniel shouted to Aaron. "Tie up that end of the log whilst I tie up this end."

Aaron dropped from the tree and ran to the log. Quick as fleas they had the two ends tied up tight.

"Oh, Dan'l," Aaron panted. "You are the durn cleverest feller this side of the ocean."

A most tremendous racket began inside the hollow log. Growls and squalls and shrieks and bellows. And the log jumped up and rolled over. It bent this way and it twisted that till Daniel thought it would surely give way at the seams.

"Oh, my body and soul!" yelled Aaron. "I never seen such a sight in my life."

By and by the log quit humping and jumping. It twisted just a little and once in a while gave a squirm. Finally it was quiet as could be and lay still. Daniel poked it cautious-like with his foot, but it never moved.

"Do you reckon the bear killed the painter?" asked Aaron. "Or was it the painter killed the bear?"

"We'll untie the log and find out," answered Daniel. "Now I'll just get my rifle ready, and you open this end of the log. Whichever one comes out, I'll be waiting to shoot."

So Daniel stood ready with his rifle-gun, and Aaron untied the log and jumped back safely behind Boone— for he knew in reason some varmint would come roaring out of there ready to eat most anything it could sink a tooth into.

But nothing came out. Nothing at all. Daniel kicked the log, and by and by a little tuft of yellow fur came floating out. And then in a spell a wisp of brown hair drifted out. Daniel rattled his rifle around inside, and finally he poked a stick into the log, but he couldn't feel a thing.

"Let's just untie the other end now," Daniel said, "and see what's going on in there."

So Aaron untied the other end, and Daniel got down on his knees and looked inside. It was mighty dark in that log. Daniel couldn't see loud thunder in there. So he got a piece of light wood and made him a torch and looked in.

Still he couldn't see anything—for there wasn't anything to see. There might have been a little more fur and what looked like part of a bear's ear and what could have passed for the very tip of a panther's tail. But that was all.

"They just eat each other plumb up," suggested Aaron.

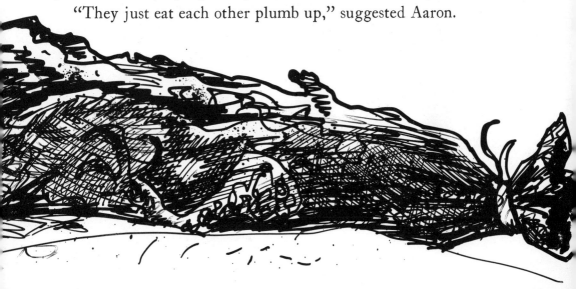

Daniel scratched his head. "That don't hardly seem logical," he said.

"Well, I reckon not, now that I come to think of it," Aaron agreed. "I ate a turkey plumb up once, but I left the bones, for my mammy can't stand to hear me crunch 'em."

Daniel studied about it a little more. "I reckon if they'd eat each other up, there'd have been a tooth or so left lying around for sure. And I don't see nary a tooth anywhere. So what I think happened was they clawed each other up into such little fine pieces they just seeped away into the air."

"Oh, Dan'l," cried Aaron. "Kentuck is certainly wonderful country, for I misdoubt that such a thing could happen in Pumpkin Grove."

"Oh, there's a heap of marvels to be seen in Kentuck," answered Daniel. "Let's build a fire and have our supper. And tomorrow we can cut logs for a cabin. And when the cabin's built, we'll travel about and see some of them marvels, for a fact."

So that's what they did. They chopped up the hollow log and built a fire out of the pieces. They cooked up some supper, and then they rolled up in their blankets to sleep.

And next morning, along about the time thrushes are first singing and the skies getting gray and 'coons are going home to bed, Aaron woke up. And he heard Daniel yell out:

"Quick, tie up that end of the log whilst I tie up this end."

Aaron sprang straight up and looked around. There was Daniel sitting up in his blankets, but Aaron couldn't see a hollow log anywhere, for they'd used the only one around for kindling wood.

He opened his mouth to ask what log Daniel meant, but instead he heard himself say, "Oh, Dan'l, you are the durn cleverest feller this side of the ocean."

Aaron most nigh fell over on his back at what he was saying, for he was mighty nigh positive it was not what he had it in mind to say. He shut his mouth and wondered how he'd managed to say all that without once moving his jaws.

And then the most awful noises started up all around him, grunts and screams and roars and snarls. Aaron knew all the varmints in Kentuck had heard he was there and had come to eat him up.

He put his hands over his ears so he couldn't hear and shut his eyes tight as could be and stood there trembling.

Four

Aaron shook so hard he stirred up the ground till he sank
down to his knees in the loose dirt.

"Oh, Dan'l," Aaron called. "I know I don't know
what to be scared of. But I believe I am learning fast,
for I can tell by the sounds this critter makes that it is
dangerous as all git-out!"

"No, no!" cried Daniel. "It ain't a thing to be feared of."

But Aaron had his hands so tight over his ears he couldn't hear a word Daniel said. "I'm ready to die," shouted Aaron. "I said my prayers. I'll die brave."

"Hush up, Aaron," hollered Daniel, loud as could be. "It ain't but an echo."

"You can have my rifle and my powder horn to remember me by," went on Aaron. "And I owe Mr. Dunkle at the trading store a penny for barley sugar. You pay him for me, Dan'l, please."

Daniel saw it was useless to try to tell Aaron what was happening, so he got up out of his blanket and mended the fire and put a kettle of water on to boil. He cut up strips of deer meat into the kettle and put in the least little pinch of salt. Then he dropped in several handfuls of meal and just a lot of Indian turnips.

By this time the noise of the fight had died down. It was quiet and pleasant and peaceful in the May woods. Daniel tasted the stew and then lay back on his blanket. He could see the new green leaves of the oak trees shining in the early morning sunlight, and he could hear the soft call of a turtle dove.

Aaron stood there waiting to be eaten. All of a sudden

he gave a big sniff, for the cooking stew was smelling mighty handsome. He opened his eyes and saw Daniel baking ash bread. He took his hands from his ears and listened carefully. There wasn't a sound of the varmint, not so much as a rabbit scrunching huckleberry leaves— just the stew cuddling down in the kettle.

Aaron looked around. His eyes got big as bowls. "Dan'l," he said, "I'll have to hand it to you. Howsomever did you manage to kill that varmint? And what have you done with its big old carcass?"

"Now sit down, Aaron, and eat," Daniel told him. "That wasn't no real live varmint. It was just an echo. This here valley we're in is powerful wide, and it just naturally takes a longish spell for the echo to get back to us. What you heard was you and me a-hollering and the bear and painter a-fighting yesterday evening."

"Well, if that don't take the rag off the bush!" Aaron exclaimed. "Folks at home will be mighty happy to hear there's such a fine echo here in Kentuckee. Leastways, I reckon they will. Though an echo ain't good for much, is it? You can't skin the critter nor eat it, can you, Dan'l?"

"Oh, there's a heap of wonders that ain't got no use to 'em," Daniel answered. "But I've a notion this here echo is going to work for us."

"Will it chop down trees and hunt for table-meat?" asked Aaron. "Will it tote our truck like a pack horse?"

"Wait and see," was all Daniel said.

All that day he and Aaron chopped logs for their cabin. Chopping down trees and trimming off the branches is hard work. After supper Aaron stretched and said, "I'm bone-weary. I reckon I'll never wake up tomorrow morning but just sleep right on through the day."

"Now don't you worry your head about that," Daniel told him. And he stood and hollered, "Wake up, boys, it's getting-up time."

"Getting-up time?" cried Aaron. "I ain't even been to bed yet. Oh, Dan'l, if this is the way things is in Kentuck, it's too fast for me, and I'm heading for home right now."

But Daniel laughed and told Aaron to get to bed and stop fretting.

And next morning, just as redbirds were whistling and the skies were turning yellow and owls were dragging themselves home to bed, Aaron heard a shout: "Wake up, boys, it's getting-up time."

"Now ain't that fine?" cried Boone, jumping up out of his blankets. "We don't need no crowing cock to wake us up, nor no blowing horn like red-coat soldiers use, for

this echo will work for us every day and rouse us up good and early. And I reckon we'll never be late now nor spend the cool of the day a-bed."

"Dan'l," said Aaron, "for a fact there ain't no cleverer feller on this green earth than you."

Aaron and Daniel worked hard all that day, and by night they had their shelter built. They were tired out once again. This time Aaron asked if he might holler out the getting-up yell.

"Go right ahead," said Daniel.

So Aaron cupped his hands around his mouth and yelled out most powerful loud, "Dan'l, Aaron says it's time to git up!" And he grinned at Daniel before he covered up with his blanket.

Daniel and Aaron lived in their little cabin, and every day they went hunting and exploring. Sometimes they went on journeys and were gone for a week or more, following a river or wandering down some valley. But they always came back to the cabin.

The calico bushes quit blooming and sarvis berries got red and ripe. Thrushes stopped singing and thunder made the cane grow tall. Aaron learned not to be scared of snakes sleeping in the sun or wood mice skittering in the leaves.

Daniel taught Aaron not to be afraid of bears or bullfrogs or hickory nuts dropping on his head. Mushrooms came poking up out of the ground, and the black gum trees turned scarlet. And Aaron found out he didn't have to be afraid of hooty owls or hailstorms or steep hills.

And every night that they spent in the cabin Aaron or

Daniel hollered out a getting-up call. And the next morning the echo hollered back, loud and clear, and woke them up.

Now one night Daniel and Aaron came back to their cabin after they'd been gone for a spell of three days. They had walked hard and fast to get back before nightfall, and they were very tired. Daniel yelled his getting-up yell, and then he and Aaron tumbled into bed and went right to sleep.

When Daniel woke up, he felt queer as a six-legged cow. Something was mighty wrong, and that puzzled him a heap. He sat up and rubbed his eyes, and then he jumped about two feet into the air.

"Great day in the morning, Aaron!" Boone cried. "Something's happened to our echo, for sure. Here it is bright noon and the sun smack overhead, and our echo's not hollered us awake."

Aaron leaped out of bed, scared as could be. "Oh, my body and soul!" he cried. "We'd best head straight home to Pumpkin Grove, Dan'l, for you know it must have been a monstrous great something that got our echo, and a monstrous great something is what I still ain't learned not to be afeared of."

Daniel took off his black hat and scratched his head, careful-like. "No," he said at last. "We must go see what happened, for I gave my word there wasn't no dreadful varmint in all Kentuck. And if there is such a varmint that has got our echo, then I must go kill it, else nobody will ever be safe in Kentuck."

"Oh, I bet it's got grisly old teeth and scaly eyeballs, and I'm scared," wailed Aaron Adamsale. "Ain't you afeared, Dan'l?"

"Aaron," said Daniel, "I've done told you and told you, a body can't be scared of something till he knows what it is. If'n you want to stay here and tremble till

47

your bones crack and never in this world know what you are trembling about, then go right ahead. But I must go."

"Dan'l," answered Aaron, "I reckon you're right as can be. And I will go with you to see what's happened to the echo. Howsomever I can't help trembling, for though I keep telling my knees not to shake, they don't pay me no mind."

It didn't take long for Daniel and Aaron to get ready for the journey. They set out across the green valley. Grasses shimmered around their knees, grasshoppers sang underfoot, and the sun shone down. And two days later they came to the banks of a river. It was too wide to swim, and it looked much too deep to ford. They made a raft of logs. Then they cut long poles and tried to shove themselves out into the stream. But hard as they both pushed, the raft wouldn't move.

Aaron jumped back on the riverbank. "I reckon a whole fistful of crawdads is holding this here raft back," he said.

He kneeled down and looked into the clear water, but he couldn't see a thing. No crawdads, no snapping turtles, no mud puppies, not even a tadpole.

He got up and dusted his knees and looked happy. "I reckon there's nothing to do but go straight back to

Pumpkin Grove," he said, "for we can't cross this river. It won't let us!"

Daniel pushed his pole back and forth in the water, and it took all his strength to move it just a little way. "I declare I believe this water is too thick," he said. "I've heared about rivers like this. Kentuckee's got so much water there ain't enough rivers to carry it off in the usual fashion. So lots of the water has to squeeze up real close together in some of the rivers, and squeezing up that way makes it mighty thick and heavy."

Aaron put a little of the water in his shot pouch to take home to his mammy.

"I expect there's enough water in this one river to make five ordinary rivers anywhere else," Daniel went on. "Well, I'll have to study on getting us across, for I've give my word and we got to get over."

Daniel considered for a spell. "Now, I believe if I ran very fast, this water would be thick enough to hold me up," he told Aaron, "for even on sunny days I am very light for my weight. But you are too heavy. I reckon you would sink."

"I could make two trips," replied Aaron. "That way I ought to be able to get all of me over."

Daniel grabbed up Aaron by his collar and the seat of

his britches and hefted the boy in his hands. "You are too heavy for me to throw all the way across," he said at last. "But I believe I could skip you over, the way a body skips a stone over water. You lay out nice and flat, and I'll try it."

So Aaron stretched out flat, but not near flat enough. Daniel had to jump up and down on him a few times to get him good and thin, and the roughest places had to be rolled out with a small log.

Then Daniel picked up the boy and threw him with just the right twist of his wrist. And Aaron hit the water just right and bounced off and hit it again a little further on and went skimming and skipping right across the river to the other side and up onto the bank.

He stood up and waved at Daniel, and Daniel waved back.

Then Daniel took a step or two backwards to give himself a running start and took out across the river. He ran as fast as he knew how, for the water was not quite as

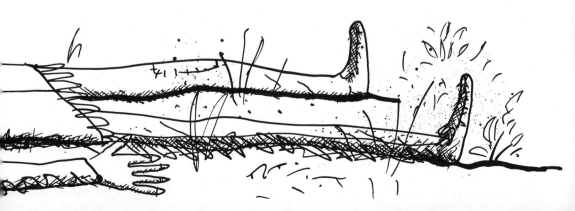

thick as he had thought and he could feel himself sink down a mite at every step.

And just as he reached the bank he stumbled and fell. Aaron reached out and grabbed him and saved him from going down in that thick old water. But Daniel's shot pouch turned upside down, and all his lead shot spilled out into the river.

"Now that is too bad," said Daniel, "for those were the finest kind of bullets. But I reckon you have aplenty, don't you, Aaron?"

"No, I don't," said Aaron, "for I threw mine out of my shot pouch so there'd be room for that heavy water I'm taking home to my mammy. I just got one lead ball left."

"Then I must make some more," Daniel told him. And he built a little fire and took a little pan and a bullet mold and some lead out of his shirt.

Aaron moved over a little closer to Daniel, for he could see something far off. "Dan'l," he asked, "what has horns, a hairy head, and raises a cloud of dust?"

"A spinning wheel," answered Daniel, for he wasn't too good at riddles.

"Well, Dan'l," said Aaron, "there's a spinning wheel coming at us from the north and a spinning wheel coming at us from the south, and I didn't have the least notion spinning wheels could look so all-fired fierce and wicked."

Daniel sprang up then. "Them ain't spinning wheels!" he yelled. "Them's buffalo, and they got us trapped between them, for a fact!"

Five

"Oh, help!" shouted Aaron. "Oh, help, help, help, helpppp!"

Now it didn't take Boone a quick wink to see that they could use some help, for the buffalo were coming straight at them, fast as a jay bird on the way to the Devil. The thick river was smack at their backs, and they had only one bullet.

And now the buffalo were so close the ground shook!

"Oh, my soul and body!" yelled Aaron. "I wisht I had me a dozen wings and a long tail, I would fly away from here right this minute."

"Now hush up and be still," cried Daniel. "Get out your knife and stand over there and hold it way up in the air."

Aaron did as he was told, for his mammy had taught him to mind folks older than he was. He looked around at those buffalo, first to one side, then to the other. The sight of those horns and those hoofs and those wicked little eyes made him wish his mammy hadn't taught him to be so mannerly.

"Hold that knife steady," commanded Daniel.

Aaron held it steady. All the time he was hollering, "Help, help, help!" but not very loud and hopeful.

Daniel now had his rifle loaded with their only lead ball. He raised the gun and aimed as careful as could be right at the knife.

Aaron shut his eyes, for he was sure Daniel had it in mind to shoot him and save him from the buffalo and he didn't want to see himself killed in cold blood.

Boone held the gun steady, right on the knife blade, and pulled the trigger. And the lead ball went whistling

through the air and hit the cutting edge of the knife
just the way Daniel meant it to. The bullet split in two,
as neat as you please. One half-bullet went north and
killed one buffalo, and one half-bullet sped south and
killed the other buffalo.

And Aaron fell flat on his back with the shock of it.

Daniel picked him up and shook a little gunpowder over him to revive him. And then they got busy and molded some more lead bullets and skinned one buffalo and had roasted tongue and fat hump ribs for supper.

Every now and then Aaron would shake all over and say, "Help!" But by nightfall Daniel had convinced the boy that he was saved and things were all right.

And the next morning early they set out again. They walked and walked, and by and by Daniel said, "I reckon we ought to be meeting up with that echo pretty soon now."

At that Aaron began to shake and shiver a little bit. They walked on and came to a place where the ground was full of sinkholes.

"Look at all them sinkholes, where the ground has sunk plumb down in the earth," remarked Daniel.

"Oh, Dan'l," cried Aaron. "You can't fool me. I know them holes are the tracks of some awful old varmint."

Daniel chuckled and kept walking. And in a spell they came to a big limestone cave. A cold wind came rushing out of it, the way it lots of times does out of caves.

"See that cave there, Aaron," pointed out Daniel.

"Now I know you are joking, Dan'l," Aaron answered, "for that's some terrible critter's burrow. I can feel it blowing its cold old breath out at me. We'd best get away from here fast."

So they journeyed along. Aaron kept thinking about sharp old teeth and thick awful paws, about fierce biting jaws and long old reaching arms, and he thought about these things till he was skittish as a gadfly.

He got so upset he ran and got in front of Daniel, for he figured he'd be safer there. But then he thought, "If any scary thing is lying in the bushes waiting for us, it will be sure to get me first."

So he scooted back behind Boone. "But now if a crawly thing comes creeping up behind, it will grab me first off and I'll never even know what chewed me up," he wailed to himself.

Then Aaron tried to walk in the middle, but it was a little hard to do with only him and Daniel there.

And now he didn't know what he'd do. But at last he had a notion. "I'll just borrow Dan'l's old black hat," he thought. "And that-a-way whatever varmint comes along will think I be Dan'l. And since the varmint's bound to swallow me first, he'll really swallow Dan'l first because he'll think Dan'l is me."

He stopped and scratched his head. "Leastways, I think that's what he'll think, though it's all a mite confusing," he added.

Anyway it was the best plan he could figure out. So in a spell he spoke up. "Dan'l, I reckon that's a fine black hat you've got there."

"Oh, I reckon it is," answered Boone.

"I reckon it must feel very fine and handsome on your head," went on Aaron.

"Oh, it does now, for a fact," nodded Daniel.

"If'n I could wear that hat for just a spell, I'd be mighty proud," Aaron exclaimed.

Daniel was a little puzzled, but he didn't say anything, just took off his black hat and handed it over to Aaron. Aaron took off his coonskin hat and handed it to Daniel, and the hunter put it on. Then Aaron put the black one on his head, and right away he felt a heap better. He felt so much better he stopped being scared and began to sing:

> *"Do-diddle-dumpty, my big gun*
> *Is the onliest, onliest, onliest one,*
> *The onliest one that I have got,*
> *And I keep it under my big black pot.*

Do-fiddle-fumpty, my big ax
Is got the biggest, widest cracks,
The biggest cracks you ever did see,
And all from chopping wood for me."

"Now you watch your step here, Aaron," said Daniel. "This here ground is full of caves and sinkholes and underground rivers. A body is liable to fall into the deepest kind of hole if he ain't careful."

"Do-diddle-dumpty," said Aaron, and Daniel took that to mean he was watching out.

They traveled on, and Aaron sang a good many songs to

keep his spirits up. But by and by Daniel didn't hear him singing any more. "Now what ails Aaron?" he wondered. "Is he shaking too hard to sing?"

He turned around to see—but Aaron wasn't there!

For a minute Boone had a sort of sinking feeling under his ribs. What could have happened to a great big feller like Aaron out here in this meadow? Where could he have got to?

"Aaron, oh, Aaron!" Daniel bawled out.

He listened hard, and in a minute he heard a faint sound.

"Dan'l, oh, Dan'l!" Aaron hollered.

"Where be you?" called Daniel.

"Oh, Dan'l, it ain't no use to look for me," moaned Aaron. "I been swallowed by some monstrous big something, and it's so dark down here in his innards I can't see a thing. Fare-ye-well, Dan'l, fare-ye-well!"

"Now just hold on a minute," yelled Daniel, and he ran toward the spot Aaron's voice seemed to come from. He had to search around a bit, but pretty soon he found it. There was a big old deep sinkhole, and down at the bottom was Aaron, stumbling around with Daniel's hat jammed down over his eyes.

"Aaron, I told you to watch out," called Daniel. "Nothing ain't swallered you. You just fell down in a sinkhole."

"I did?" asked Aaron. "In a sinkhole?" He felt around over the wet rocks and earth that lined the sinkhole. Then he stopped and thought a minute. "Well, then I been struck blind, Dan'l, for I can't see my hand behind my face."

It was all Daniel could do to keep from laughing at Aaron. "Oh, you just got my old hat pulled down over your eyes," he told him. "Take it off and I'll see about getting you out of there."

Aaron put his hands up and tried to pull Daniel's hat off his head. But it was stuck fast. Aaron pulled and tugged and kicked and cussed a little. He said, "Dang!" and he said, "Ding!" and he said extra loud, "Blast my grand-daddy's old green saddlebags!"

Then Aaron gave up, for he saw he would need Daniel's help before he could see again. "Get some vines and throw 'em down to me," he hollered up at Boone, "and pull me out quick."

Daniel looked all around that big meadow. He could see grass and clover and one lone button bush and that was all. No trees, no vines, no deer antlers, nothing to help a body out of a hole.

"Aaron," he called at last. "There ain't no vines around here. There ain't nothing. Danged if I can see how we're ever going to get you out of that hole!"

Six

Well, when Aaron heard that, he was mighty taken aback. He sat down and wiped a few tears off his chin and tried to be brave.

"Dan'l," he called finally. "You reckon I got my full growth yet?"

"Oh, I don't know," replied Daniel. "How come you to ask, Aaron?"

"Well, I figure in a year or two, maybe I'll just grow out of this hole, Dan'l," said Aaron.

"Now, that could happen sure enough, here in Kentuck," Daniel told him. "And that puts me in mind of how I got out of a sinkhole once. It wasn't far off from this very place neither. I was out by myself and it was dark, getting on for night. It was raining too, raining 'coons and 'possums, so I couldn't see a thing. And suddenlike I fell down in one of these here holes. Well, I lit at the bottom with nary a scratch or broken bone, and I made up my mind there wasn't a thing I could do for myself till daylight. I had some corn in a poke, and I ate a handful for my supper. I dropped a few grains, but I never thought nothing about it at the time. I just snugged down in my blanket and went on to sleep. And the next morning, you know what?"

"No, I don't," said Aaron and wiped off another tear.

"Them grains of corn I dropped had took quick root and sprouted and started growing, and I never knew a thing about it. I was sleeping right on top of them sprouts, and they just pushed me on up with 'em. And when I woke up the next morning, me and that corn was up out of the sinkhole and twenty feet above the ground. It gave me something of a shock when I saw where I was. And that corn was still a-growing too, so I skinned down a stalk right quick, I can tell you. It just goes to show you what Kentuckee dirt and water will do for a grain of ordinary corn."

"Oh, Dan'l, drop some corn down here quick," cried Aaron.

"Now, Aaron, you know all the corn I got has done been ground up into meal," said Daniel. "It wouldn't work."

"Well," sighed Aaron, "I guess there ain't nothing for us to do but set here two, three years till I grow some."

Daniel scratched his head. "There's just one thing wrong with that scheme," he called down to Aaron. "If'n you stay here, I got to stay here too to feed you and take care of you, like I said I would. And I just ain't got two, three years to spare right now."

"Oh, I wisht I could get this hat off," exclaimed Aaron, "for if I could see, I know in reason I could think of a way to get out of here."

"Well, try again," urged Daniel.

So Aaron grabbed the hat and pulled with all his strength. He jerked and hauled and shoved at that hat until he lifted his feet clean up off the ground!

"Try harder, Aaron!" cried out Daniel.

And Aaron blew out his cheeks and gathered up his

67

muscles and tried one more *tree*-mendous try. He gave such a push at the hat that he lifted himself right up out of the hole! Daniel grabbed him as he came up and pulled him safely onto firm ground.

"Oh, Aaron," cried Daniel, "that was quite a thing to do. I have seen a little light feller lift himself up by his boots, but I never before knowed a big heavy body like you that could hoist himself plumb up in the air like that."

"Well," said Aaron gloomily, "I ain't strong enough to get this fool hat off, I know that."

Daniel led Aaron to a creek and soaked his head for a spell, hoping the cold water might shrink the boy's head a mite. But Aaron said he'd just as soon be blinded by a hat as drownded by a creek. So Daniel made a poultice of slippery elm bark and put it on the hat, but that didn't help either.

Daniel was mighty provoked because there were very few problems he couldn't figure out if he put his mind on them. And he knew there was some way to get this hat off Aaron if he could just think of it.

He thought about cures for sheep rot and recipes for herb tea and ways to keep rifles from rusting, but none of them seemed the right thing to do for a small hat on a large head.

At last Aaron said, "You'd best git out your knife and cut it off, Dan'l."

"What!" squalled out Daniel. "Cut up my old black hat? What would I drink out of? What would I mix my gunpowder in? What would I carry honey in or boil salt in or sleep under on cold nights? No-sirree-William-tail-saw-horse, I won't never cut up my old black hat!"

Now that made Aaron a little mad, for he was tired of not being able to see anything but the inside of an old black hat. So he sat down to sulk a bit. And while he was sitting there, Daniel came tippy-toeing up behind him, quiet as a snowflake.

And when he was right behind Aaron, he let out a most dreadful yell. It was part panther-scream and part Shawnee war-whoop and part buffalo-bellow, with just a mite of rattlesnake-rattle thrown in for good measure.

Aaron's hair stood right up on top of his head. And his hair going up like that just naturally pushed the hat clean off his head. It sprang a good ways up in the air, and Daniel caught it as it came down. He put it on his own head and handed Aaron the coonskin cap.

"That wasn't any varmint hollering," Daniel told the boy kindly. "That was just me. So put on your fur hat and let's be on our way."

Aaron was so scared his knees wouldn't bend, and he had to walk stiff-legged for several miles. In spite of that they made pretty good time, and by nightfall they had come almost the whole way across the valley. Daniel felt sure in the morning he could find out what had happened to his echo. But he didn't say anything to Aaron for fear of scaring him.

"Let's make camp right here," said Daniel.

And Aaron nodded, for though he'd got his knees to working, his jaws were still pretty stiff with fright and he couldn't say much.

They cooked up some supper and ate it. Then they bedded down, and just as Daniel was beginning to snore, Aaron poked him.

"What's that big thing crouching over there, Dan'l?" whispered Aaron. "Look at what big old shoulders it's got. And oh, look at them hateful old spines all over it."

Daniel looked. "Why, that's just a mountain," he told Aaron. "And them ain't spines, them's pine trees. Now go to sleep!"

"Oh, Dan'l, you can say that, for you ain't seen it rolling a big yeller eye around, the way I have," moaned Aaron. "Oh, Dan'l, ain't you never heared tell of the One-Eyed Glut? This here is it, for folks has always said it has big old poisonous spines that make you swell up and turn blue if you touch 'em. Oh, it's a most terrible varmint! The very mention of its name makes little babies in their cradles holler like they had the colic."

Daniel looked again. And he saw the clouds blow by and the moon come rolling in sight. "That ain't no yeller eye," he said. "That's the moon shining down on the mountain. Now go to sleep afore I put the kettle over your head to keep you quiet."

Aaron had had enough things over his head for one day, so he did as he was told. And the next day he woke up and saw the mountain with the pine trees on it, and he was a little bit put out with himself for having made such a fool mistake.

"Now, Aaron," said Daniel. "We'll get over to that mountain, and I believe then we'll find out what happened to that echo."

Aaron went off by himself and loaded his rifle with a double portion of powder and lead. He was ashamed to let Daniel see him doing it.

They set out and soon reached the mountain. It was covered with the biggest monstrous trees Daniel most ever saw.

"My body and soul!" exclaimed Aaron. "I've seen a heap of big trees, but I've never seed the likes of these."

"Well, look at that one yonder at the bottom," Daniel said.

Aaron looked, and there was the hugest old sweet gum tree in all creation. Its great old knotty limbs sprangled out in all directions. Prickly sweet gum balls as big as Aaron's two fists hung from the twigs. And a few star-shaped leaves, purple and brown, still clung to it. And all down one side of the trunk a whole river of sweet gum glistened and sparkled.

"Don't it smell sweet?" asked Aaron. "And oh, wouldn't my mammy love to see all that amber-gum? That's enough to cure all the coughs in Caroliny, I reckon."

Daniel stared at the gum. There was a funny-looking place where something fluttered weakly, as though an insect or bird was caught there in the resin. "Aaron," he said, "I believe that's our echo caught in that gum."

But Aaron didn't dare look. He kept his rifle ready, just in case a Glut tried to spring at them.

Boone climbed up the trunk till he was high enough to get at the echo where it was stuck. And he took out his knife and stretched out his arm careful-like so as not to get caught in the sticky gum himself, and he cut the echo loose. It was weak and thin from having struggled so long to get free, and when Daniel hacked it out of the gum, it broke in two.

Half of it rolled off among the rocks saying, "Dan'l-anl-nl-lll." And the other half flapped off into the trees saying, "Wake up-kup-kppp." And that was the end of it.

Daniel climbed down and cleaned off his knife. And Aaron stood there with his head hanging. "Oh, Dan'l, you were right," he said at last. "All them awful creatures I was so scared of, they all turned out to be nothing at all. I've trembled and shook till my ribs are most nigh disjointed. I've shivered something awful about a monstrous big varmint, and there ain't no such thing here."

"Oh, Aaron," cried Daniel. "You have learned what not to be afraid of, for the very most important lesson is that a body must first go and see what a thing is before he gets scared of it, else it's a great waste of time and trouble, shivering over what isn't there at all."

So Daniel and Aaron went back to their cabin. They stayed there all winter, hunting and exploring and enjoying themselves, and using a new echo to rouse them out of bed of a morning.

Spring came, and pink and yellow moccasin flowers bloomed. Snakes shed their skins, and wagtails flew up and down the creeks. The poplar trees blossomed, and it was May.

Aaron and Daniel walked through Cumberland Gap and down the trail to Pumpkin Grove. Evan Dunkle sprang up out of the bolts of cloth and bags of gunpowder when he saw Daniel's old black hat and Aaron's coonskin cap.

"Oh, Aaron!" he shouted. "Are you safe? Have you got all your fingers and ears and elbows? Has some monstrous big Sumpple taken a bite out of you somewheres where it don't show?"

And everybody came rushing out of the trading store to see Aaron and to poke him and pinch him and to be sure he was safe and all in one piece.

"Aaron, did you see a One-Horned Sumpple?" asked one man.

77

"Oh, yes," said Aaron. "I seen a heap of them. They make powerful good eating, and they are easy to kill. You just make a mean old face at 'em, and they fall dead with fright."

"Did you see a Sling-Tailed Galootis?" asked another man.

"Oh, yes," said Aaron. "There was so many of them I had to shake 'em out of my blanket at night. They was too little to be worth killing, though."

"Did you see a One-Eyed Glut?" asked a third man.

"Oh, yes," said Aaron. "I only saw one. It had got tangled in some brier thorns and wore itself to death trying to pull loose."

"Aaron," said Evan Dunkle, "are you trying to tell us there ain't no monstrous big somethings in Kentuck?"

"Oh, Evan," cried Aaron. "There are monstrous big trees and monstrous big bears and monstrous big valleys and rivers. But there's not one thing for a man to fear in Kentuckee. The place to be afraid is in Pumpkin Grove, where you can't see all them varmints, but can only set and tremble a-thinking about 'em."

"Then let's go to Kentuck with Dan'l," cried Bill Sickles.

Daniel smiled to see the men go rushing off to get their

wives and young 'uns, their pots and quilts, to take to Kentuck.

He chuckled to see the red bird sitting in the top of the poplar tree. He laughed to see rabbits go jumping over the huckleberry bushes, for 'way far off, he seemed to hear a small voice saying, "Let's go, Dan'l; it's getting-up time!"